MR. TEMPKIN CLIMBS A TREE

This **PJ BOOK** belongs to

_____

_____

PJ Library®

JEWISH BEDTIME STORIES and SONGS

IN MEMORY OF MY GREAT UNCLE, ISAAC (ITCHA) STRICKER —C. F.

KAR-BEN PUBLISHING, INC.
A division of Lerner Publishing Group, Inc.
241 First Avenue North
Minneapolis, MN 55401 USA
1-800-4-KARBEN

Website address: www.karben.com

Main body text set in Mikado a.
Typeface provided by HVD Fonts.

Library of Congress Cataloging-in-Publication Data

Names: Fagan, Cary, author. | Arbat, Carles, 1973– illustrator.
Title: Mr. Tempkin climbs a tree / by Cary Fagan ; illustrated by Carles Arbat.
Other titles: Mister Tempkin climbs a tree
Description: Minneapolis : Kar-Ben Publishing, [2019] | Series: Kar-Ben favorites | Summary: When elderly Mr. Tempkin's plan to thwart the squirrels that have been raiding his birdfeeder goes awry, his neighbor Marky learns how special a friendship can be.
Identifiers: LCCN 2018032668| ISBN 9781541521735 (lb : alk. paper) | ISBN 9781541521742 (pb : alk. paper)
Subjects: | CYAC: Old age—Fiction. | Friendship—Fiction. | Neighbors—Fiction. | Jews—Fiction.
Classification: LCC PZ7.F135 Mp 2019 | DDC [E]—dc23

LC record available at https://lccn.loc.gov/2018032668

PJ Library Edition ISBN 978-1-5415-7911-8

Manufactured in China
1-47181-47898-1/17/2019

071929.2K1/B1415/A6

MR. TEMPKIN CLIMBS A TREE

CARY FAGAN

ILLUSTRATIONS BY
CARLES ARBAT

KAR-BEN
PUBLISHING

I'm sitting on the porch, counting my trading cards, when Mr. Tempkin walks by on his way home from synagogue. He lives alone in the house next to ours. As usual, he waves to me.

"Hi, Marky," says Mr. Tempkin. "Ready to help?"

"Ready!" I say.

"Mr. Tempkin, how old are you?" I ask as I come down the porch steps.

"Not as old as Rip Van Winkle," chuckles Mr. Tempkin, "but I'm getting close."

My job is to water all the flowers in Mr. Tempkin's garden. Mr. Tempkin fills the bird feeder. The birds twitter impatiently. As soon as Mr. Tempkin's done, they swoop down and start eating.

"Look, Marky. A cedar waxwing!" Mr. Tempkin says, pointing.
I stare at the beautiful bird. I've never noticed a bird like this before.

Dad says that spending time with Mr. Tempkin is a mitzvah, and
if it is, it's a fun one, because I really like Mr. Tempkin.

Mr. Tempkin suggests I pull up weeds.

"Is it hard to be old?" I ask as I work.

"Sometimes," Mr. Tempkin says with a nod.

"But there are four things that keep me going."

"What things?"

"The first is walking to synagogue every morning.

"The second is smelling my roses.

"The third is listening to the birds.

"The fourth is you!"

"Me?"

"There's nothing like having a friend," Mr. Tempkin says.

"You're good company, Marky."

The next morning Mr. Tempkin comes out onto his porch and waves as usual. I jump up and go over to help him.

Mr. Tempkin is in a huff.

"Those pesky squirrels keep raiding my bird feeder. I'm going to have to hang it higher up, where they can't reach it."

Mr. Tempkin ties a rope to the bird feeder and starts climbing.

"Mr. Tempkin, aren't you too old to climb a tree?" I ask.

"Nonsense!"

Mr. Tempkin climbs higher and higher.
"I think this is far enough," he says. "I'm
getting a little dizzy up here."
"Maybe you should come down," I suggest.
"I just have to tie this rope to the end of the branch."

Mr. Tempkin reaches out and ties the rope to the branch.
But suddenly . . .

. . . he loses his balance. Mr. Tempkin falls through the branches and leaves. He lands on the ground with a **whump!**

I run over. "Are you okay, Mr. Tempkin?"

"I'm fine, Marky... except for my ankle.
I don't think I can stand up."

"Don't move, Mr. Tempkin!" I say. "I'll be right back!"

I run into my house. "Mr. Tempkin fell out of his tree!" I tell Mom. She calls for an ambulance on her cell phone as she hurries outside.

The paramedics carry Mr. Tempkin to the ambulance on a stretcher. "So much fuss for nothing," Mr. Tempkin sighs.

I watch the ambulance go down the street.

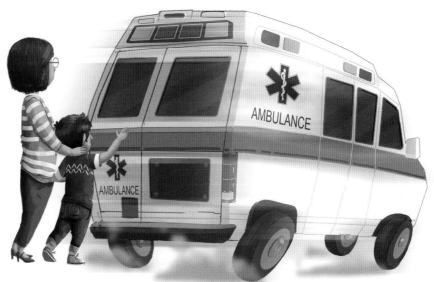

All day I wait for Mr. Tempkin to come back.
I eat my lunch on the porch. I read books.
I watch the birds.

Finally a taxi pulls up in front of Mr. Tempkin's house.
The driver takes a wheelchair out of the trunk. He helps Mr. Tempkin get out of the car and into the wheelchair. There's a brand-new bandage on Mr. Tempkin's foot. "Don't worry, Marky, it's just a sprain," he says. "I need to keep this bandage on for two weeks so it'll heal properly."

I breathe a sigh of relief. "I'm glad nothing was broken!"

"Me too! Climbing trees is not for old men, and I guess I'm just a foolish old man," he says.

"No you're not," I blurt out. "When I'm old I'm going to climb trees, too!"

Mr. Tempkin laughs.

"What time is it?" Mr. Tempkin asks, looking at his watch.

"I think I can make it to synagogue for the afternoon service. See you later, Marky."

I watch as Mr. Tempkin pushes himself along in his wheelchair.

But he only goes a few feet before he slows to a stop.

"I guess I'm just not strong enough," he says.

"Maybe I can push you," I offer.

Mr. Tempkin's eyebrows go up. "Better ask your parents."

My mom says that helping Mr. Tempkin would make me a mensch. I get behind the wheelchair and grab the handles. Mr. Tempkin grasps the big wheel. Together we move along the sidewalk. "Teamwork!" cries Mr. Tempkin.

At last we get to the synagogue. "Isaac Tempkin!" says the rabbi as we enter. "What happened to you? And hello, Marky! Nice to see you."

"I fell out of a tree," said Mr. Tempkin. "Isn't it nice that my friend Marky helped me to get to the synagogue today?"

The rabbi smiles. He gives me a kippah to put on my head. The service begins.

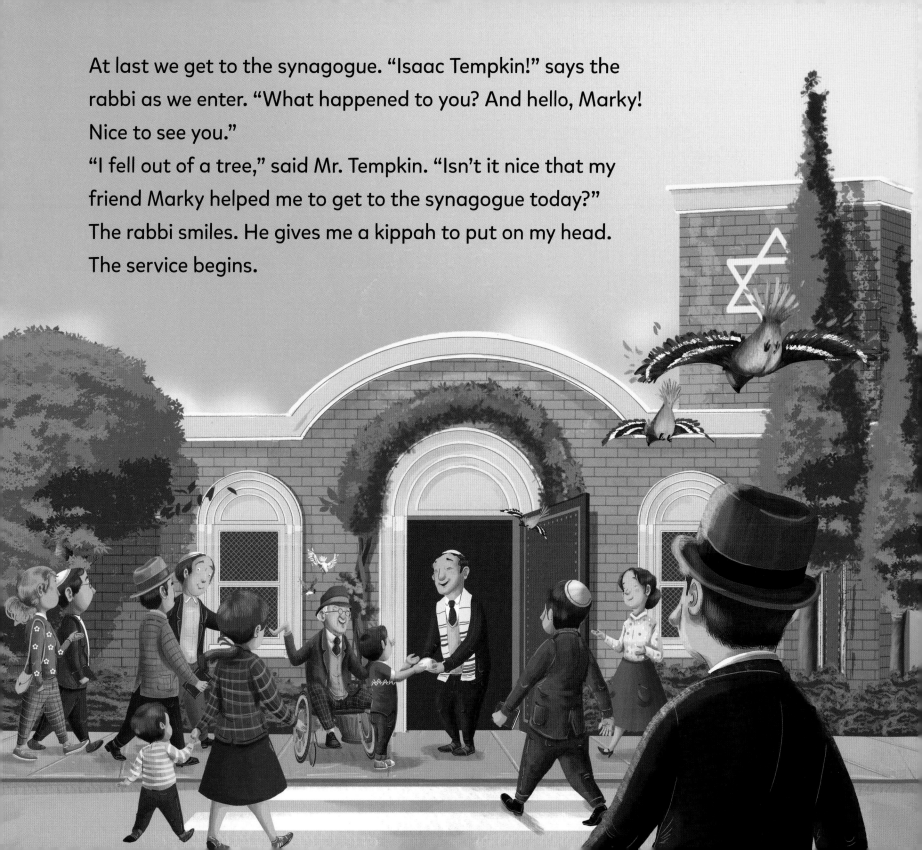

Mr. Tempkin and I wheel home again.

"You must be tired," says Mr. Tempkin, "pushing me all that way."

"I'm fine," I say. "Now I'm going to take care of the garden."

Mr. Tempkin sits in his wheelchair as I work. "Let's give a little more water to those roses," he says.

The bird feeder is too high for me to reach.
"No climbing," Mr. Tempkin says. "This time we'll
use our heads."
We find a small bucket and tie it to the end of a
broomstick. Mr. Tempkin fills the bucket with birdseed,
holds it up, and pours the seed into the feeder. The birds
immediately fly down.
"Look, blue jays!" says Mr. Tempkin.
We both grin.

Every morning I help push Mr. Tempkin to the synagogue and back again.

Two weeks later Mr. Tempkin goes to the hospital for a checkup. I sit on the porch waiting for him to come back.
A taxi brings Mr. Tempkin home.
He gets out—without his bandage! He does a little dance.
"Hurray!" I shout.

Time for school. Mom and Dad watch from the porch as I get on the bus.

Mr. Tempkin comes outside.

"Now it's *my* turn to wait for *you*," he says with a wink.

As I climb onto my school bus, I can hear the birds singing. Mr. Tempkin is right.

There's nothing like having a friend.